DOUBLE TROUBLE!

Sarah Dyer

This is Ellis

and this is Erin.

No, wait!

This
is
Ellis

and
this
is
Erin.

They are **twins!**

Erin **loves** to climb,

share toys

and is **excellent** at puzzles.

Ellis **loves** to eat,

be creative

and jump **really** high!

But
what they
both love
doing
is . . .

. . . looking for **trouble!**

Trouble can be found

almost **anywhere** in the house

so the **twins** head upstairs to the attic.

"Ummmm, it's a bit **dark** up here!" says Ellis.

"Here's a torch" says Erin helpfully.

"I can't see trouble up here . . .

only **s . . . s . . . spiders** lurking in the corners!"

Next, they check the bathroom.

"No, I don't think **trouble's** here" says Erin.

The bedroom
is **filled**
with
lots and **lots**
of things,

but
not
trouble.

They **look** in every cupboard and corner,
but can't find **trouble** in the kitchen.

The **twins rummage** through the bags and boxes in the garage.

"**Trouble** isn't here" says Erin peeking under the car.

After **searching** the house from top to bottom,

the **twins** rush outside.

"**Trouble** sometimes climbs into bins"

says Ellis **confidently**.

"**Nope**, not in here" **shouts** Erin, "not even right at the bottom!"

"Maybe,

trouble

is waiting for us

    up this **big** tree?"

says Ellis.

    "**No**, not up here,

    not even if I climb

        really high."

"I don't think you'll find **trouble** there," **sighs** Erin.

"**Hang on!** I know where **trouble** might be . . ."

"In this muddy

puddle!" the **twins** shout with glee.

Trouble still hasn't shown up,
so they decide to sit and wait.

"**Trouble** might come and look for us!" Ellis winks.

"Yes,

especially if we pretend we're not watching",

whispers Erin.

Suddenly, Erin thinks of a new

hiding place for **trouble.**

"Hellooooooo?"

"Trouble, are you down there?"

she calls out.

When they get no answer from the hole,
they **look** around for something else to do.

"Perhaps **trouble** is **playing** with Buddy?" suggests Ellis.

"**Nope**, I can't see trouble here!" **giggles** Ellis.

"**Ewwwww**, me neither!" **shrieks** Erin.

Feeling disappointed that they couldn't find **trouble.**

The **twins** head back to their bedroom.

Bored of looking for **trouble**,
they decide to make a **pirate den** instead.

"I have the **flag!**" cries Erin.

"**Look!**" points Ellis

"**Trouble** has been hiding under our noses all this time!"

"**Yipee,** we found . . ."

"TROU

TROUBLE

BLE!"

This is Ellis

and **this** is Erin.

and **this** is their cat, **Trouble!**

She often goes **missing** and can be **very** hard to find.

"You didn't think **we** were going to get **in to trouble** . . . . **Did you?**"

For Eden x x x

With special thanks to **Beast the Cat** for the inspiration.

First published 2019 by order of the Tate Trustees
by Tate Publishing, a division of Tate Enterprises Ltd,Millbank, London SW1P 4RG
www.tate.org.uk/publishing

Text © Tate Enterprises 2019
Illustrations © Sarah Dyer 2019

A catalogue record for this book is available from the British Library

ISBN 978 1 84976 659 3

Distributed in the United States and Canada by ABRAMS, New York
Library of Congress Control Number applied for

Colour reproduction by DL Imaging, London
Printed and bound in China by C&C Offset Printing Co., Ltd

FSC
www.fsc.org
MIX
Paper from
responsible sources
FSC® C008047